This book belongs to

_____

_____

For Granny Mary,
Mum and Ellie
S.G.

First published in Great Britain in 2008 by

Gullane Children's Books
185 Fleet Street, London, EC4A 2HS
www.gullanebooks.com

10 9 8 7 6 5 4 3 2 1

Text and illustrations © Sarah Gibbs 2009

The right of Sarah Gibbs to be identified as the author
and illustrator of this work has been asserted by her in
accordance with the Copyright, Designs and Patents Act, 1988.
A CIP record for this title is available from the British Library.

ISBN: 978-1-86233-626-1   hardback
ISBN: 978-1-86233-775-6   paperback

Printed and bound in Indonesia

Monsters Are...

Sarah Gibbs

GULLANE CHILDREN'S BOOKS

There are lots
of **monsters** in the
world and they are all
different...

Some **monsters** are **messy...**

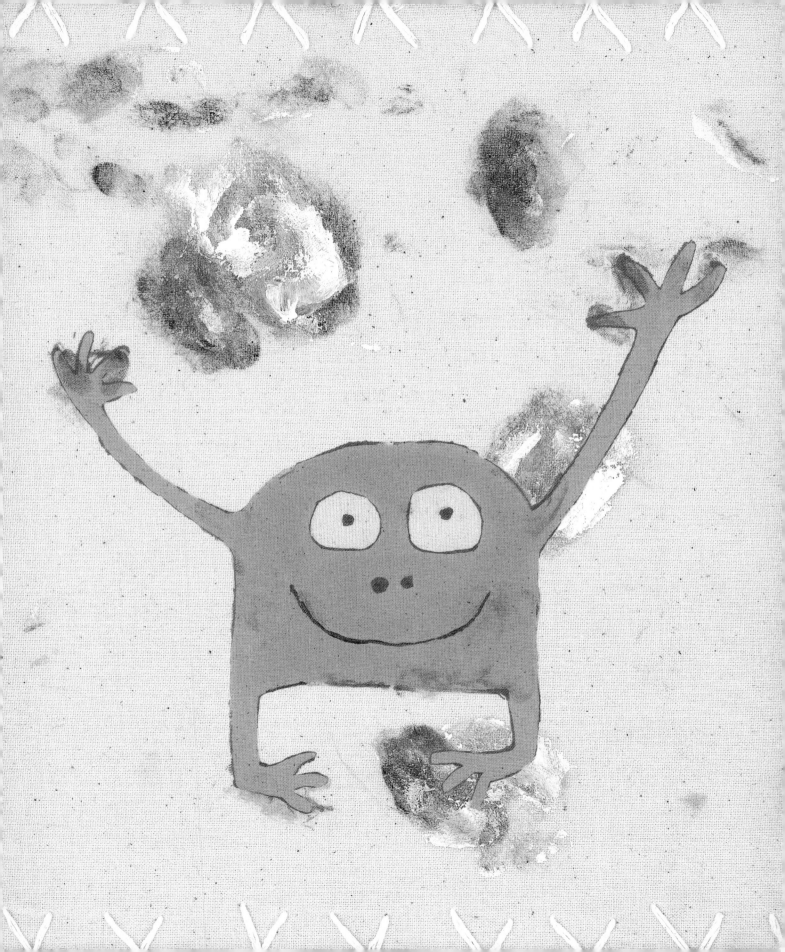

And some

monsters are

pretty ugly!

Some **monsters** like to blend into the **background** . . .

Others don't!

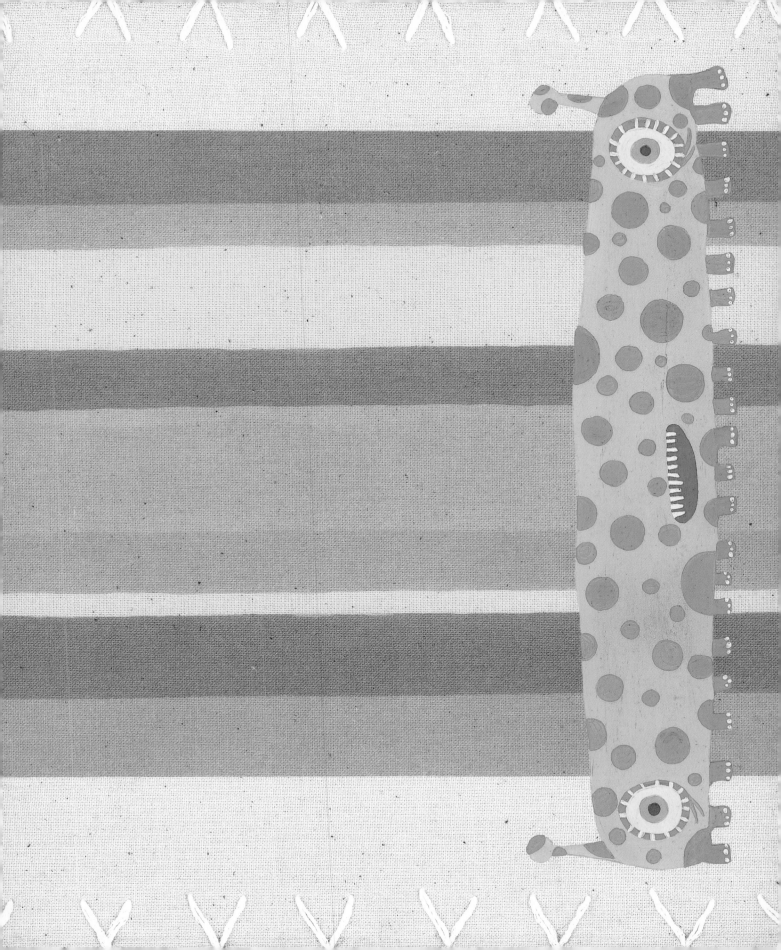

Some
monsters
talk
rubbish...

And some have

bad
breath!

Some **monsters are** small . . .

But they all have

BIG

friends!

Some **monsters** steal **socks...** and sometimes **pants!**

And some **monsters** only come out in the **DARK...**

But when the night starts to fall . . .

And it's
time for bed . . .

Mum says that's when **I'm** the **biggest** little **monster** of them all!

Other Gullane Children's Books for you to enjoy . . .

Tabitha's Terrifically Tough Tooth
Charlotte Middleton

Holly's Red Boots
Francesca Chessa

Blame it on the Great Blue Panda!
written by
Claire Freedman
Illustrated by
Emma Carlow & Trevor Dickinson

Billy Bean's Dream
Simone Lia

Small Florence
Claire Alexander